MW01104631

ANNA'S GOAT

for Anna Kozicka Simon

for Wanda Kozicka Syrowinska

and in memory of Leon and Lucyna Kozicki

JKK and JW

Illustrator's Note

The main illustrations were executed on colored paper with Conté crayons. I would like to acknowledge the many photographs of Roman Vishniac, which were helpful in my research. Many thanks to Bubblegum and the staff at the Toronto Riverdale Zoo, and to all the friends who modeled, including Jenny the goat.

Text copyright © 2000 Janice Kulyk Keefer
Illustration copyright © 2000 Janet Wilson

No part of this book may be reproduced, stored in a retrieval system, or transmitted, in any form or by any means, without the prior written permission of the publisher or, in the case of photocopying or other reprographic copying, a licence from CANCOPY (Canadian Copyright Licencing Agency), 6 Adelaide Street East, Suite 900, Toronto, Ontario, M5C 1H6.

Canadian Cataloguing in Publication Data
Keefer, Janice Kulyk, 1952–
Anna's goat

ISBN 1-55143-153-X

1. World War, 1939–1945—Refugees—Juvenile fiction.
I. Wilson, Janet, 1952– II. Title.
PS8571.E435A76 2000   jC813'.54   C00-910551-4
PZ7.K22563An 2000

First published in the United States, 2001
Library of Congress Catalog Card Number: 00-104250

Orca Book Publishers gratefully acknowledges the support for our publishing programs provided by the following agencies: The Government of Canada through the Book Publishing Industry Development Program (BPIDP), The Canada Council for the Arts, and the British Columbia Arts Council.

Cover design by Christine Toller
Printed and bound in Korea

IN CANADA:
Orca Book Publishers
PO Box 5626, Station B
Victoria, BC Canada
V8R 6S4

IN THE UNITED STATES:
Orca Book Publishers
PO Box 468
Custer, WA USA
98240-0468

02 00 00 • 5 4 3 2 1

160885

ANNA'S GOAT

written by Janice Kulyk Keefer

illustrated by Janet Wilson

ORCA BOOK PUBLISHERS

FAR, FAR AWAY, across the plains and over the mountains in a cold, dark country, Anna was born.

She was a red, tiny, helpless thing, but when her sister Wanda put her finger into Anna's fist, the baby held on beautifully tight. Watching their daughters holding hands, Mother and Father smiled the way a new moon smiles in the evening sky. They almost forgot the war that had driven them so far from home.

When she was feeding Anna, Mother would tell Wanda all about the wonderful city they would return to one day, when it was safe for them to live there.

Such beautiful parks and palaces, with trees making tall green fountains all along the boulevards, and cafés where you could eat little cakes topped with spun sugar. Wanda would chew on a crust of rye bread, baby Anna would curl and uncurl her tiny toes, and Mother's face would become a rose blooming in the winter sun.

For it was always winter in the faraway place where Anna was born. There was hardly any wood to burn to keep their one room warm, and hardly any food to eat. The grownups had to work at the factory all day to help the soldiers who were fighting for them in the war.

Life was very hard for Anna's mother. Her husband was sent to live in another village, and there was no one to help her care for her children. One morning, she found she had no milk left to give her baby. She rocked the crying Anna in her arms, thinking hard and deep, with her eyes shut tight as buttons, until she knew exactly what to do.

That day, when she went to the factory, Mother spoke to the village women who worked beside her. They too were very poor, and had children of their own to feed. But when they saw how small and hungry this baby was, they nodded their kerchiefed heads together and told Anna's mother they would help her. Mother thanked the women and gave them a bundle of clothes to take home to their children.

That night there was a knock at the door. When Anna's mother opened it, what should walk inside but a strange creature with four skinny legs, a fat, fleecy coat and a beard like a curl of cloud! Wanda stared and stared, and then looked up at her mother, asking the question just with her eyes.

"This is a nanny goat," Mother answered. "She will stay with you and Anna when I go to work. All day you can cuddle up beside her, and when I come home each night, I will milk the goat for your supper."

And indeed, all through that dark, cold time, the
goat kept the children safe and warm and full as
summer. Wanda grew taller, and Anna changed
from a baby who was always sucking her thumb …

... to a little girl who laughed when the nanny goat tried to eat, not just hay, but spoons and candles and even towels dancing on the washing line!

One evening, when Mother was resting, Anna tried to pour herself a cup of milk from the stove and burned herself. Mother bundled Wanda onto a sled and ran with Anna in her arms all the way to the hospital, with the nanny goat trotting after them. When Anna went to sleep at last, with her head and hands wrapped up in bandages, her goat lay down beside her. Anna could feel the warm, strong heartbeat through the tangled fleece.

It was a bitter time, and a hard, hard place, but at last one day the war was over. Anna and Wanda and Mother and Father packed up their belongings to begin the long journey home. But they could not take their nanny goat all the way over the mountains and across the plains, back to their own country. For the village women needed her milk for their own children now, and they promised to take loving care of Anna's goat.

At long last, after traveling all through spring
and long past summer, Anna's family came home.
But home had vanished. The parks and palaces,
the trees and cafés of Mother's stories, had been
bombed into rubble, along with the schools and
playgrounds. The whole city had to be built up
again, brick by brick.

Somehow, people managed. No one had much of anything but hope that life would be better one day. And so, while their parents worked at rebuilding their city, the children would play house in the piles of rubble all around them.

If only there was a treasure you could find in the heaps of wood and stones. Something strange and perfect you could hold in your hand, like the glint of a star — something that would keep on shining, even in the dark. All the other children found pennies or beads or bits of painted china, but Anna could never find anything wonderful enough to keep.

"Mama," she cried when she came home again with empty hands. "Everyone has found a treasure — everyone but me!"

Mother looked at the bare, bare walls around them and hugged sad Anna in her arms. She thought deep and hard, shutting her eyes as tight as buttons, until she knew exactly what to do. And then she ran to the cupboard, opened the door and pulled out a small blue towel with a fringe on the end.

Anna took the towel in her hands, trying not to cry. How could this raggedy cloth be a treasure? It was so plain, and half of the fringe was missing. "Anna," said her mother, raising Anna's chin with her hand, "don't you remember your nanny goat?"

As Anna listened to her mother's story of the faraway place where they had lived during the war, she held on tight to the towel. She began to remember the cups of rich, warm milk she'd held in her icy hands, and the strange, living softness of a pillow of fleece. When her mother had finished, Anna looked up and asked her a question, just with her eyes. Her mother stroked Anna's hair and said, "Of course you may have it, my dear, dear Anna."

And that is how Anna found a treasure of her very own to keep. She would lie in bed each night with her face pressed against the corner of the towel where the fringe had been. She would think of the school where she and Wanda would go one day, the school rising brick by brick from the rubble. She would think of how she'd been born so far away, over the mountains and across the plains, in a place where it was always winter.

And as she fell asleep, she could feel, like a bright, strong star in her hands, the heartbeat of her nanny goat.

GIBSON ELEMENTARY
11451 - 90th Avenue
Delta, B.C. V4C 3H3

When she grew up, Anna made her home in Canada. She lives in a stone house in a little village by a river, and she sculpts wonderful things out of clay — birds and suns and mermaids ...

... and nanny goats, of course!